IN THE NIGHT KITCHEN

MAURICE SENDAK

HARPER & ROW, PUBLISHERS

FOR SADIE AND PHILIP

DID YOU EVER HEAR OF MICKEY, HOW HE HEARD A RACKET IN THE NIGHT

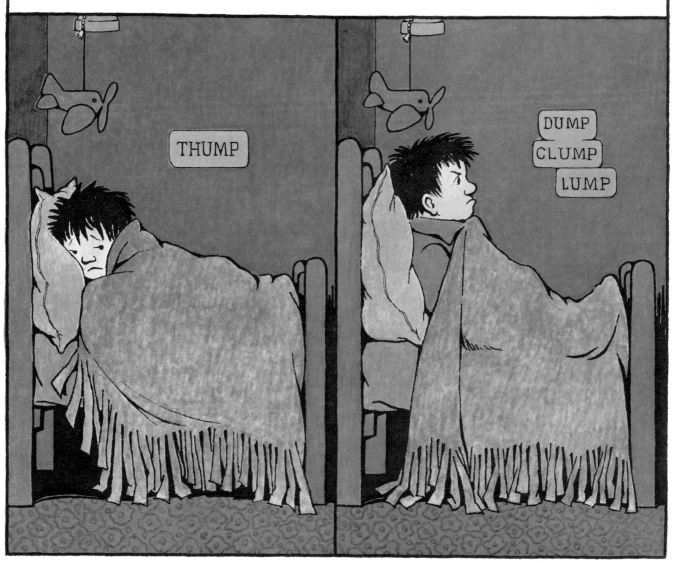

AND SHOUTED

QUIET DOWN THERE!

WHERE THE BAKERS WHO BAKE TILL THE DAWN SO WE CAN HAVE CAKE IN THE MORN MIXED MICKEY IN BATTER, CHANTING:

AND THEY PUT THAT BATTER UP TO BAKE

A DELICIOUS MICKEY-CAKE.

SO HE SKIPPED FROM THE OVEN & INTO BREAD DOUGH
ALL READY TO RISE IN THE NIGHT KITCHEN.

MICKEY THE MILKMAN DIVED DOWN TO THE BOTTOM

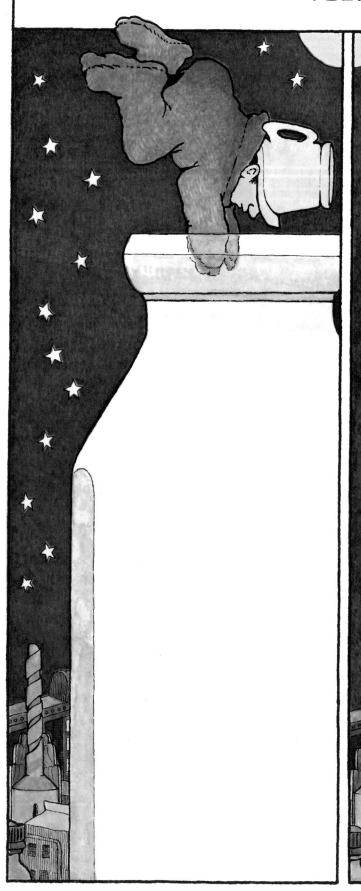

SO THE BAKERS THEY MIXED IT AND BEAT IT AND BAKED IT.